Copyright
© 2021 by Vern
Kousky • All rights reserved.
Published in the United States by
Random House Studio, an imprint of
Random House Children's Books, a division
of Penguin Random House LLC, New York.
Random House Studio and the colophon are
trademarks of Penguin Random House
LLC. • Visit us on the Web! rhcbooks.com
Educators and librarians, for a variety
of teaching tools, visit us at
RHTeachersLibrarians.com   Library
of Congress
Cataloging-in-Publication
Data is available upon request.
ISBN   978-0-593-17342-8   (trade)
ISBN   978-0-593-17343-5 (lib. bdg.)
ISBN   978-0-593-17344-2   (ebook)
The text of this book is set in 20-point font
Brandon Grotesque. The illustrations
were rendered in mixed media,
digitally assembled.   Book
design by Rachael Cole

MANUFACTURED IN CHINA
10 9 8 7 6 5 4 3 2 1
First Edition

Milo is Missing Something

vern kousky

RANDOM HOUSE STUDIO ▪ NEW YORK

Milo hatches,
then yawns and stretches,
and opens his curious eyes.

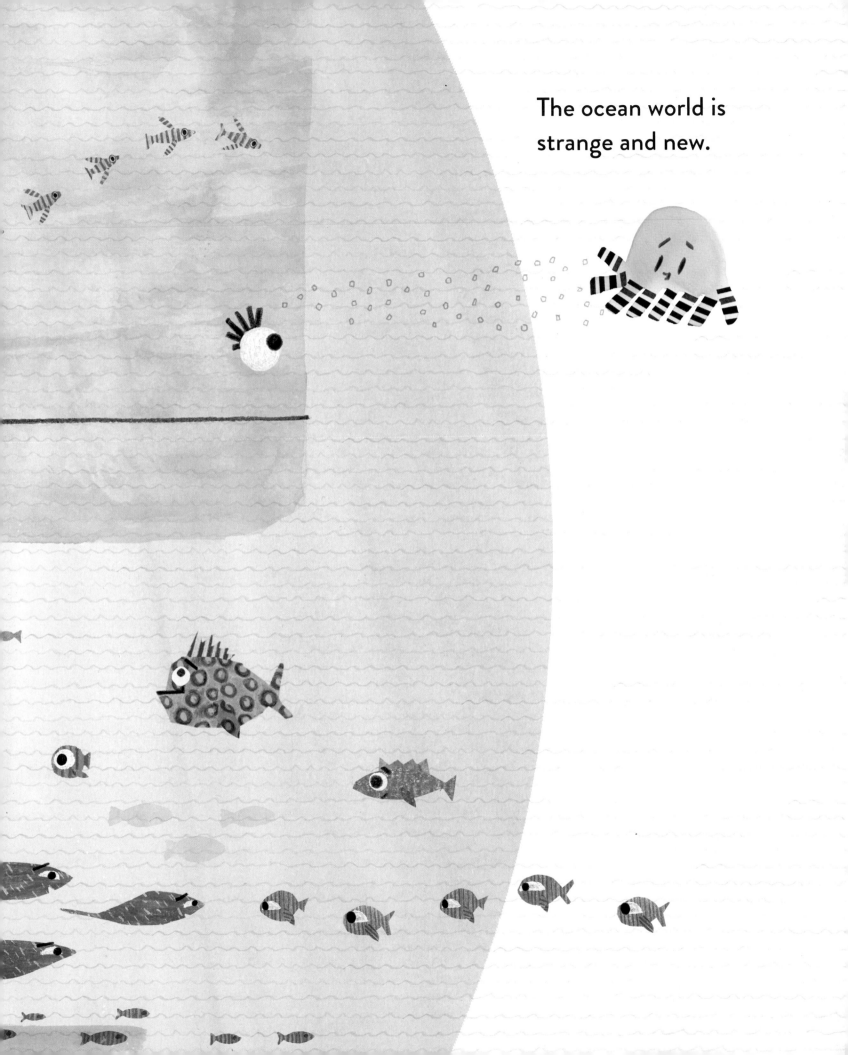

The ocean world is
strange and new.

The coral reefs, so colorful.

The deep sea caves
are dark and cozy.

So what is
Milo missing?

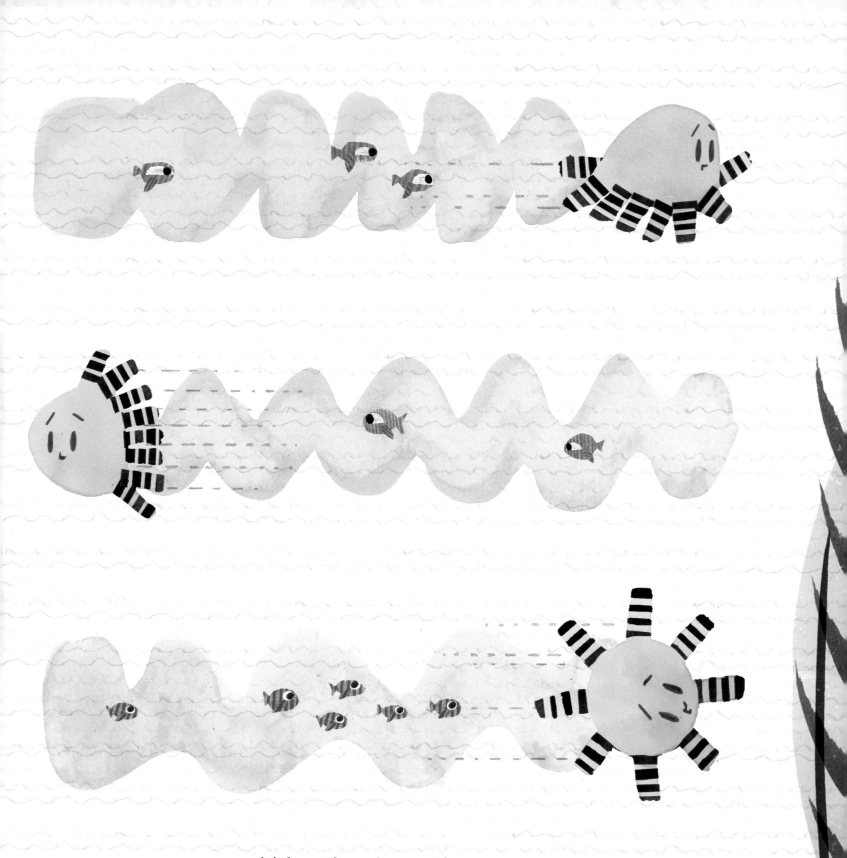

Milo rides the swift sea currents,

plays hide-and-seek with
some hungry sharks,

shhhh

finds sunken treasure in an old shipwreck.

Now what could
there be missing?

NO
SWIMMING!!

What fun! What fun!
Milo's learned to walk.

To the tide pools
he goes exploring.

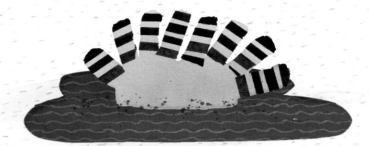

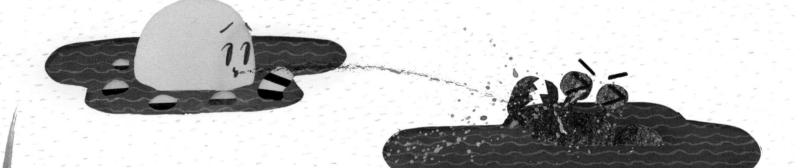

The water here is
warm and calm.

Yet there's something
still that's missing.

Milo makes
a friend
down deep.

And look—he's
made one more!

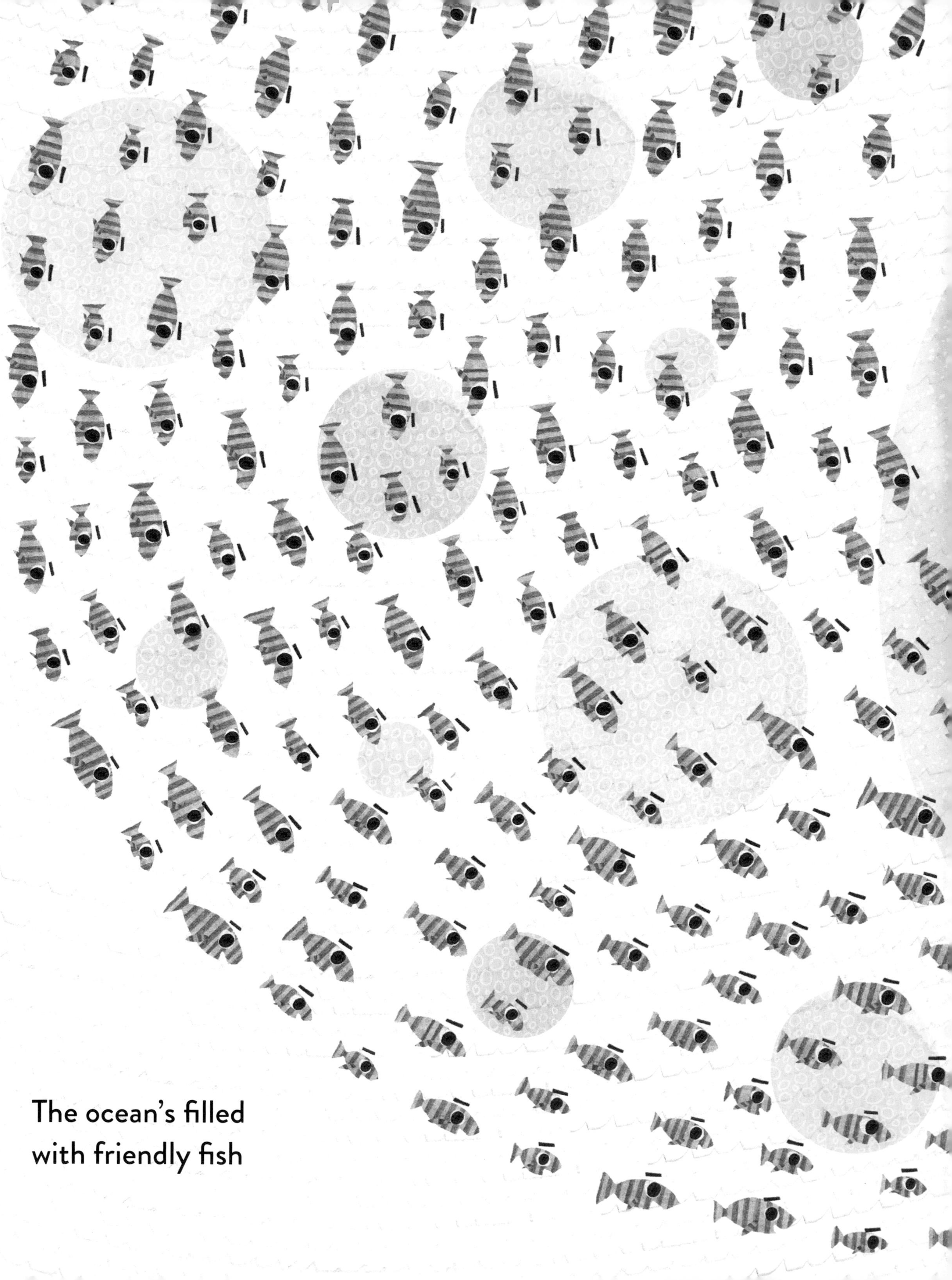

The ocean's filled
with friendly fish

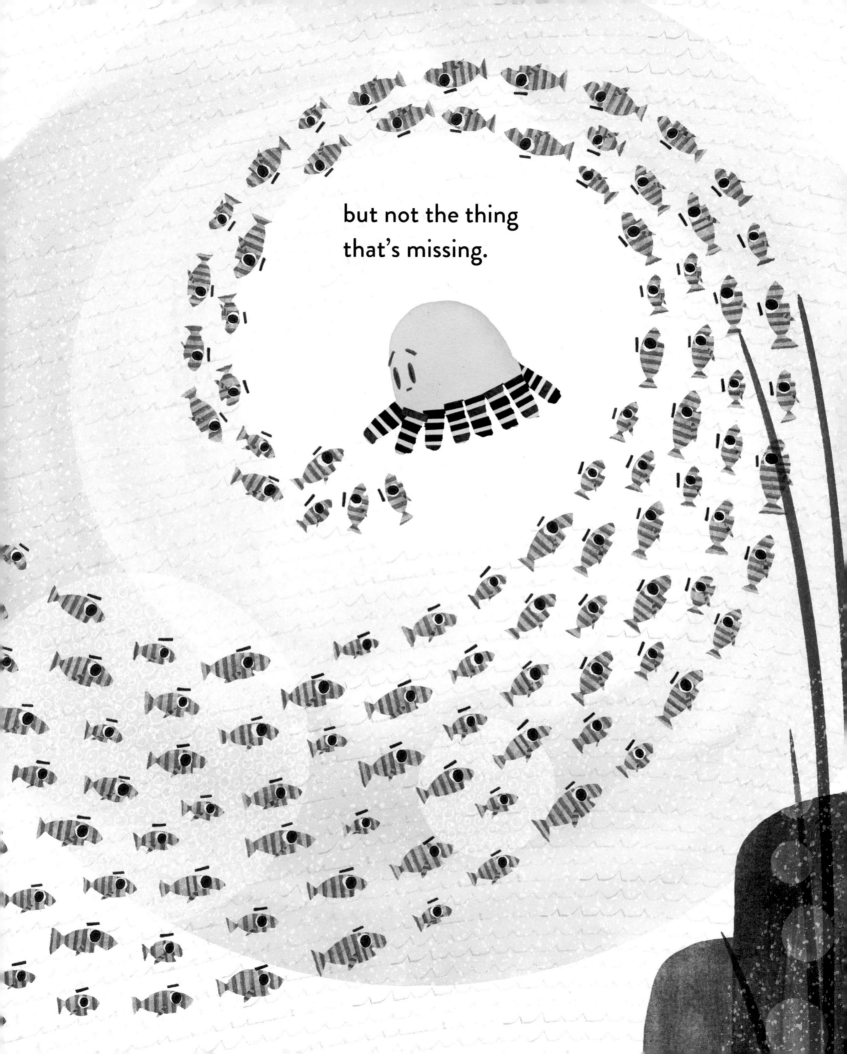

but not the thing
that's missing.

Milo searches
from shore

to shore,

from the surface

to the inky
bottom.

He knows it's out there,

but he knows not where,

the thing that must be missing.

Milo is sleepy. He can search no more.

So he sleeps alone on the ocean floor

and dreams he's found what he's been
searching for,
the thing he's sure is missing.

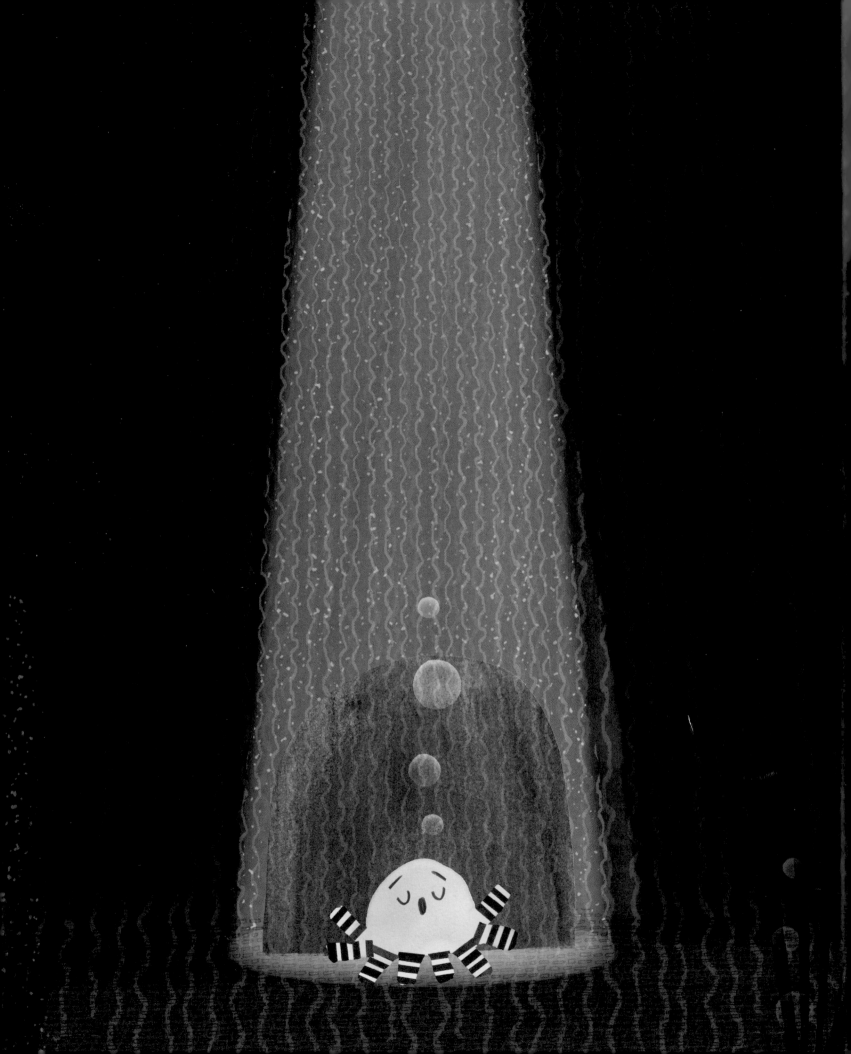

Milo wakes, alone no more!
His family has found
him on the ocean floor.

At last, he knows what
he's been searching for.

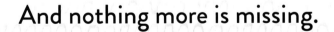

And nothing more is missing.